The Limit of Reality: A Dance Between the Real and the Spiritual

Chowikei Studio

Published by Chowikei Studio, 2024.

The Limit of Reality

© 2024 Chowikei Studio

For more information contact:
Chowikei Studio
chowikeistudio@gmail.com
www.chowikei.com

Table of Contents

Dedication

To my mother, who taught me that beyond what we see, there are invisible forces that shape our lives. Thank you for always reminding me of the importance of energies, cleansing the soul, and maintaining the balance between the positive and the negative. This story is inspired by your wisdom and those little mysteries you have always believed in. May blessings and light follow you wherever you go.

Foreword

Ever since I was a child, I have felt that there is something beyond what we can see or understand. My mother once told me that our grandparents were of indigenous descent, which sparked in me a deep curiosity about what happens after death. Over the years, I have researched various religions and listened to paranormal stories, merging what I have heard into a single narrative. What you are about to read is not a true story but is inspired by accounts I have collected and transformed into this fictional journey. Although some experiences may seem familiar to those who have had paranormal encounters, this story is still a work of fiction.

Chapter 1

Invisible Inheritances

Since time immemorial, some families have carried an invisible legacy, an inheritance found not in documents or wills, but in the whispers of past generations. These families were bearers of an inexplicable connection with what cannot be seen, with what dwells beyond the tangible world. Stories of shadows, of echoes in the night, of blurred figures that moved in the shadows without a trace. For most, these stories were legends, but for certain families, they were part of their reality.

The ancestors of many of these families were no ordinary people. They were said to be able to talk to spirits, to know the secrets of wind and fire, and to know how to interpret the hidden signs of nature. They performed rituals to protect themselves from bad energies, lit candles to guide the lost dead and burned sacred herbs to cleanse the air of dark presences. These acts were not superstition to them; they were survival. They knew that, if they did not take precautions, what lurked in the shadows could cross the threshold of their homes.

These families lived in the balance between two worlds: the visible and the invisible. At first glance, their lives seemed normal. The children ran through the fields, and the adults worked the land or sold their produce at the market, but there was always something more. On the darkest nights, when the wind came through the cracks in the windows, the stories came to life.

The elders said that some people were born with the "gift" or "sixth sense," a link to what most could not perceive. For these people, the boundaries between the living and the dead, between the here and the hereafter, were thinner, they sensed the energies in the places they visited, knew when a presence was unwelcome, and sometimes had premonitions that alerted them to what was to come.

In families with generations of this legacy, spiritual knowledge was transmitted in silence, in kitchens, around campfires, or while caring for the sick. Grandmothers taught granddaughters to clean the home not only with soap and water but with herbs and prayers so that negative energies would not remain. Grandparents knew how to read the signs of the wind and warned about the days when the air brought more than just the change of season.

In these families, all was not peace. They knew that the gifts also carried a burden. Those who could see beyond were often haunted by shadows that wanted to trap them. Fear of the unknown was constant, but they accepted it as part of their lives. Over the years, these experiences have become normalized. But now and then, something so strange, so frightening, that even those who were accustomed to the paranormal were shaken.

Over time, some of these families began to move away from their spiritual roots. New generations, more modern and technology-focused, ignored the teachings of their ancestors. But some could not escape their legacy. Even if they tried to lead a normal life, something always called them back. A recurring dream, an inexplicable feeling of being watched, or the constant echo of voices in their ears.

One of these families, although not fully aware of it, was destined to face the echoes of the past again. The family of Diana and Alejandro. Although they were trying to lead a common life, away from old beliefs, destiny had in store for them a reunion with their legacy. A legacy that had been dormant for generations, waiting for the right moment to awaken.

Diana, without knowing it, was one of the heirs of that gift, of that connection that ran through her family's veins. Since she was a little girl, she had had strange dreams and visions that she could not explain, but she had never paid much attention to them. Her mother, more practical and modern, preferred not to talk about such things. But her grandmother's stories, and legends about her great-great-grandparents, always haunted her mind, especially when shadows seemed to move in her room at night.

Now, however, the past was about to catch up with them.

Chapter 2

The Journey

Diana remembered the times when her grandmother would make her sit on her lap and talk to her about the spirits that protected the family and the need to keep the aura clean. She had taught her simple rituals with salt and holy water to ward off bad energies. Although at the time, Diana didn't fully understand what they meant, as she grew older, she began to experience little glimpses of what her grandmother had spoken to her about.

Her dreams, for example, often seemed to predict situations that would later occur similarly in real life. What puzzled her was not so much the coincidence between her dreams and reality, but the growing sense of familiarity she felt with the unseen world. When she shared these experiences with her mother, her mother simply smiled and advised her not to obsess about such things. Her mother preferred to focus on the present and not on what lay beyond the veil.

On the other hand, Alejandro, her older brother, shared that curiosity, although from a more logical perspective. Always analytical, he was inclined to look for scientific explanations for what Diana was experiencing, and although he did not completely rule out the paranormal, he preferred to keep his feet on the ground.

It was Alejandro who had suggested the idea of the trip to Mount Prisank. They did not want to go to a typical tourist destination; they were looking for a place with history, with legends. Something that would allow them to experience something different, something that few dared to explore. When they found Mount Prisank in an old guidebook of mysterious places, they were both intrigued. The mountain had a reputation for unexplainable events, and both Diana and Alexander felt it was the perfect place for their getaway.

As they traveled into the bush, the excitement was palpable. Diana, Alejandro, her mother, and two close friends, Laura, and Sofia, were talking about what they might find there. The journey was made pleasant with stories and laughter, but something in Diana would not let her relax completely. Since they had left the city, she felt a pressure in her chest, as if something was watching her from afar.

-Mom, there's something special about this place," Diana commented as they got out of the car at the gas station, halfway up the mountain. -You're right," her mother replied. I don't know if I like what's special about this place, though. There's something in the air... different.

An old man at the station, watching the new arrivals, approached slowly, his face marked by years. -Mount Prisank holds secrets that it is better not to awaken," he said, in a raspy, mysterious voice, before walking away without giving any further details.

The man's warning only increased Alejandro's curiosity and Diana's restlessness. But the idea of exploring such an enigmatic place fueled her desire to discover something deeper, something the old man's words seemed to confirm.

-Did you know that legend has it that Mount Prisank is cursed? -commented Alexander, breaking the silence as he gazed at the mountain in the distance.

-Yes, but don't you think all that is just to attract curious tourists? -replied to Sofia, with an amused tone.

-I don't know," Diana interjected, "I feel that there is something special about this place, something that is not just a legend.

Their mother turned from the front seat and smiled at them, downplaying the conversation.

-Let's just enjoy the ride, guys. It's quiet and remote, that's what counts.

When we arrived at the cabin, the atmosphere changed. The coolness of the place contrasted with the warmth of the car, and the shadows of the trees seemed to lengthen more than usual. Diana felt a shiver but attributed it to travel fatigue. As they unloaded the suitcases, Alejandro approached her.

-Are you all, right? -he asked.

-Yes, just tired, I think," Diana replied, not mentioning the restlessness that had followed her since they had started the trip.

The cabin was in a secluded area, surrounded by dense forest and only a few miles from the bush. It was perfect for a quiet getaway, but it also had that mysterious air that Diana couldn't ignore. In the evening, after settling in, they decided to light the fireplace and enjoy a simple dinner.

-This place is more impressive than I thought," said Laura, looking out the large windows overlooking the forest.

-Impressive, but also somewhat disturbing," added Diana, as she curled up in a blanket.

The conversation drifted to ghost stories and local legends. Alexander mentioned some of the stories he had encountered about Mount Prisank, about people who had mysteriously disappeared, and others who claimed to have seen strange figures in the forest.

-What if we find something tomorrow? -Laura asked jokingly, but with a spark of curiosity.

-Whatever we find, we will face it together," said Alejandro, trying to instill confidence in everyone.

Diana was silent, but inside she knew that this trip would be different. The stories her grandmother had told her were beginning to echo in her mind, and the feeling that something was moving in the shadows was growing stronger. She couldn't know it yet, but something in Mount Prisank had awakened, and this trip would be more than they had imagined.

Chapter 3

The Mountaineers

The sky over Mount Prisank was clear that morning. The first rays of sunshine caressed the hut where the group had spent the night. Diana awoke with a strange feeling in her body as if the mountain was calling her somehow. But she attributed it to the chill of dawn and the excitement of the trip.

-Ready for the adventure? -asked Alejandro, already at the door of the cabin with a loaded backpack and a smile from ear to ear.

-More than ready," replied Valeria, adjusting her gloves and hat.

The day promised to be perfect for a long hike, exploring, and enjoying the views. Diana, Alejandro, Valeria, and the rest of the group began to climb the first trail with renewed energy. The giant trees and fresh air filled the atmosphere with a tranquility that made them forget any worries.

-I didn't think the mountain was so impressive," said Laura, looking up at the tops of the pine trees that seemed to touch the sky.

-It's incredible. -Diana smiled, enjoying the moment. Although that strange feeling she had had in the morning still lingered, she didn't let it bother her.

The walk was what they had expected: a pleasant stroll, amid laughter and light conversation. From time to time, Alejandro would point out some interesting plant or rock, giving small explanations. The tranquility of the place and the fact that it was so far away from civilization made everything feel almost magical.

-Look! -shouted Valeria suddenly, pointing to a hut that looked like a shelter that was barely distinguishable among the trees. Shall we go and see what that is?

Just before they could respond, they saw a group of mountaineers coming out of the hut. They looked normal, dressed in hiking clothes, and were walking in the opposite direction from Diana's group.

-Did they come from the cabin? -asked Laura, curious.

-It seems so," said Alejandro. It looks like a shelter, let's look at it and see what's interesting about it.

The group stopped in front of the hut, which appeared to have been neglected, despite having seen the mountaineers leave. It was surrounded by a wild garden, and its roof, covered with moss, was barely holding up.

-It looks like it hasn't been cleaned," said Alejandro, opening the wooden door with a slight creak.

Inside the cabin there was little more than old furniture, a few kerosene lamps, and a fireplace with damp wood. There was nothing out of the ordinary, but something in the atmosphere seemed off. Diana noticed two backpacks on the table, she thought they belonged to the mountaineers they had seen in the distance.

-Who would have left them here? -asked Laura, approaching with curiosity. Maybe it belongs to a group of mountaineers.

-Perhaps they leave them here to climb to the top of the mountain without much weight and pick them up on the way back," commented Alejandro, although his tone reflected a slight doubt.

Suddenly, a dull thud, like a knock, echoed behind them. The four turned in unison, expecting to see something or someone, but there was nothing. Only the wind was rustling the branches of the trees, creating eerie shadows on the ground.

-It must have been the wind," said Valeria, trying to play it down.

Diana, however, could not shake the strange feeling she had had since they entered the cabin. Something was not right. Though she tried to push those thoughts away, the atmosphere felt heavier than usual.

-Shall we go on? -asked Laura, heading for the door.

The group left the cabin and continued their hike. As they went on, the forest around them grew colder because of the altitude, but the day was still clear and calm.

-Who would have built that cabin? -It feels like someone built it for a living and then left it to tourists.

-They were probably families of mountaineers who lived here many years ago," answered Alejandro, although inside he also felt his sister's concern.

They continued walking along the trail, which was getting steeper by this point. The views of Mount Prisank were spectacular, with the sun shining on the snow-capped peaks in the distance. Everyone was quiet, sometimes tired, taking selfies with their phones, laying down for a while to rest, drinking a little water, and continuing the hike.

A while later, they found a middle-aged man, dressed in a ranger's jacket, standing at the edge of the road, watching the horizon.

-Hello," shouted Alejandro, approaching the man, "Are you from the area?

The ranger nodded and approached the group with a friendly smile.

-Yes, I've been working on this mountain for years," he replied, with a slight local accent.

-We found a hut further back like a shelter to rest, but some people left some backpacks in there. Do you know anything about it? -asked Diana.

The ranger's face changed immediately as if he remembered something unpleasant. His eyes narrowed, and his tone became more serious.

-That cabin... -he said cautiously. Many years ago, a group of mountaineers disappeared in that area. No one knows what happened to them. Their belongings were left there, but they never returned. Some people like you see them leaving the hut.

The group exchanged glances, feeling a palpable discomfort in the air.

Do they never find their bodies? -asked Valeria, with a tone of disbelief.

-No. They've never been heard from again," the ranger replied. Sometimes hikers report seeing strange lights or hearing noises near that cabin, but there is no explanation.

Silence fell over the group. No one said anything, but they all felt the same: there was something about that mountain that they didn't quite understand.

-Well, be careful out there," added the ranger before walking away. The mountain has its mysteries.

The group continued their walk, but the atmosphere was no longer the same. The laughter had died down, and the weight of the story they had just been told hovered over them. Diana couldn't stop thinking about the lost mountaineers they had seen about those backpacks that had been left there as a reminder of something they still didn't understand.

In the distance, the sound of the wind blew again, and for an instant, she swore she heard a faint whisper that made her stop in her tracks. But when she looked around, all was silent, as if the mountain itself was watching them, waiting for their next move.

15

Chapter 4

Shadows on the Mount

The sunrise on Mount Prisank was a mixture of pale and cool tones filtering through the pines. The group awoke with the idea of making the most of the day; Alejandro had planned a hike that would take them to explore beyond the cabin. Diana, Laura, and Sofia were a little nervous about the stories Alejandro had told the night before, but the adventurous mood still prevailed.

-Come on, girls, this is the day to climb to the top of the mountain. -Alejandro adjusted his backpack energetically, ready for the hike.

Diana, although she tried to stay positive, couldn't help but feel a nagging uneasiness since they had arrived. Her grandmother had always told her about the "feeling in her stomach," that pressure that indicated something wasn't right. She felt it now but attributed it to nerves and the strange atmosphere of the place.

The morning was clear, but the air was thick and cold, charged with something they could not identify. Alexander led the way, map in hand and the confidence of one who believed himself invincible. The trails on Mount Prisank were not marked, and that gave it a touch of mystery that further fueled the group's expectations.

-Ready for the big adventure? -asked Alejandro, looking back as the group followed close behind. Diana tried to smile, but the feeling in her chest wouldn't let her.

-This place is... strange," commented Sofia, as she looked at the trees around them. I don't know if it's my imagination, but I feel that something is following us.

Laura laughed, playing it down. -It's just the magic of the place. Besides, this is perfect for some dreamy photos.

As they walked, the group moved deeper and deeper into the forest, and the shadows cast by the trees seemed to move strangely. Alejandro, ever the optimist, paid little attention to the girls' concerns.

The wind whistled through the branches, creating a sound that chilled Diana's blood. She stopped for a second, trying to identify where the noise was coming from.

-Did you hear that? -he asked, turning his head quickly.

-Just the wind, Diana. Don't worry," answered Alejandro, without pausing.

But something inside her told her it wasn't just the wind. She felt a presence, something watching her from the shadows. Diana tried to shake off that feeling, concentrating on the path, and following in her brother's footsteps.

As they ascended, the air became thicker, as if each step they took immersed them in an atmosphere of another time. The trees grew taller and taller, and the sound of their footsteps echoed in the void as if the mountain was waiting for something.

-What if we took a shortcut? -suggested Laura, tired from the climb. We could return earlier and have time to rest and take more photos.

Alexander looked at the map and then at the darker trail leading into the bush.

-That shortcut isn't on the map, but... -he smiled, unable to resist the temptation. It might be more interesting.

Diana, who had already felt an increase in the pressure in her chest, hesitated. She looked toward the path and then at Alejandro but decided not to say anything. She didn't want to look like the one who was always afraid.

With each step they took, the forest became denser, and the sunlight barely penetrated the treetops. Diana felt something closing in on them as if the forest was enveloping them in darkness.

Suddenly, the whistling came again, this time louder and clearer. Diana stopped dead in her tracks, her heart pounding.

-Alexander, please tell me that was the wind too," she whispered, hoping that her brother would give her a reassuring answer.

But Alejandro did not respond immediately. He turned to her, with a more serious expression than usual.

-Maybe... I don't know. -Her voice no longer sounded so confident.

The group stopped, listening to the sound. It was a high-pitched whistling sound that seemed to move through the trees, changing direction, as if it were circling them. Diana felt a shiver run down her spine. Her instinct told her they were not alone.

Sofia, who had been quiet for much of the tour, took Laura by the arm.

-I don't know about you, but I don't feel safe here," she muttered, looking around with a mixture of fear and distrust.

-Maybe we should go back to the cabin," suggested Diana, finally expressing the fear that had been plaguing her since they began the walk.

But Alejandro did not want to give up. He was determined to go further, to explore the unknown.

-Just a little more. I'm sure we'll find something amazing," he said, trying to keep up the adventurous spirit of the group.

Diana followed but couldn't shake the feeling that something was wrong. As they walked deeper into the forest, the shadows seemed to come alive, moving around her, closer and closer. She felt that they were watching her, stalking her.

She stopped for a moment to adjust her scarf and braids, and when she looked up, she realized she was alone. The group had moved on without her.

-Alejandro! -he shouted, his voice echoing in the cold air, but there was no response.

Panic began to take hold of her as she looked around. The path she had followed was no longer clear, the shadows were lengthening, and it seemed that everything had changed in a matter of seconds.

-No, it can't be," she muttered to herself, trying to calm down.

She turned again, looking for some trace of her friends, but the forest enveloped her completely. She tried to walk back, but it seemed that the same path she had come on now disappeared into the trees. The pressure in her chest increased with each step.

-Hello? -he called, his voice trembling. -Is anyone there?

The wind blew again, carrying a soft murmur, almost like a whisper. Diana stood still, her breath hitching, trying to decipher the words she thought she heard. But there was no one. Only the shadows seemed to move among the trees.

She began to walk faster, desperate to find her way back. Every crunch under her feet made her jump, and she felt something following her, always out of sight, but present. The trees were closing in on her, and the sky, which had once been clear, was now covered by a thick layer of gray clouds.

The clearing she reached offered her no solace. The feeling of being watched intensified, and fear paralyzed her. She looked around, searching for some sign of life, but found only more shadows, more darkness.

-God, please let this be a bad dream," she murmured, hugging herself to try to calm down.

The wind blew once more, carrying with it a high-pitched whistle that faded into the trees. She was alone, lost, and something was watching her from the shadows.

Chapter 5

The Encounter with the Elderly

Diana slowly joined the group. Her shaking hands reached for the canteen in her backpack as she wiped her eyes, trying to clear her mind of the overwhelming sensation she had felt. She took a sip of cold water, thankful that her friends were waiting for her a little further down the trail. Laura was the first to approach.

-Are you all, right? -he asked with concern, offering her a hand.

-Yes, I just... I got a little dizzy," Diana replied, trying to sound convincing, although the fear still lingered inside her.

Alejandro watched from a distance, arms crossed, and one eyebrow raised.

-Are you sure you want to go on? -We can come back if you feel bad," his brother asked.

Diana shook her head, though her stomach was still churning from the experience. She couldn't explain what she had felt, but she didn't want to appear weak to her brother either.

-I'm fine," he said more firmly. Let's move on.

The group resumed their march, moving along the narrow path that led deeper into the bush. The air was heavy and the forest, in its stillness, felt more ominous. Every step she took seemed to rumble on the ground, and although the company of her friends should reassure her, the feeling of being watched did not leave her.

-There's something strange about this forest, don't you think? -asked Valeria, breaking the awkward silence.

-It's just the altitude and the fatigue," Alejandro replied, although even he sounded less confident.

As they advanced, the terrain became more rugged. Branches crunched under their feet, and the air felt thicker.

Diana noticed that the trail was beginning to veer off into a part of the forest that seemed darker, almost as if it were shrouded in permanent shadow. She clenched her fists, trying to remain calm, but something inside her screamed that they should not continue down that path.

-Maybe we should go back," he finally said, no longer able to contain his fears.

-We haven't come this far to turn back now," Alexander replied with a defiant smile, although his gaze showed some doubt.

It was then that Diana felt it again: the pressure in her chest, the sensation of the air getting thicker, and the cold that crept into her skin despite the sun shining through the trees. He looked up and, as he did so, spotted a faint light through the trees. It was not the warm light of the sun, but a cold, distant flicker.

-See that? -he muttered, stopping dead in his tracks.

The group turned their heads, following his gaze. In the distance, in the gloom of the forest, a figure loomed in the shadows. It looked like a person, but the distance and the fog distorted its features. Alexander frowned, but before he could say anything, Diana began to walk towards the figure, as if something beyond her comprehension was drawing her.

-Diana! -shouted Laura, but Diana didn't listen. Her steps took her directly toward the figure, and the air around her grew colder with each step she took.

When she was close enough, she could see the old woman. Her brown skin was wrinkled with age, but there was wisdom in her dark eyes. She was dressed entirely in white and wore colorful necklaces around her neck, and in one hand she held a lit tobacco. The smoke formed spirals that floated in the air, creating a surreal atmosphere around her.

-What are you doing here, child? -asked the old woman, her voice deep and full of mystery.

Diana tried to respond, but the words would not come out of her mouth. The woman's presence had left her paralyzed.

-I've been waiting for you," said the old woman, slowly approaching her.

The rest of the group watched from a distance, unable to move. It was as if time had stopped as if the encounter between Diana and the old woman was taking place in a space apart from reality.

-Who are you? -Diana managed to ask, her voice barely a whisper.

The old woman did not respond immediately. She took a deep puff of her tobacco and exhaled the smoke calmly. Then, with a gentle gesture, she motioned for Diana to follow her.

-Come. There are things you need to know," he murmured, in a voice that was more of a command than an invitation.

Diana, feeling a strange confidence in that figure, followed her without hesitation. The old woman led her deeper into the forest, towards a small opening in the ground, a path hidden in the undergrowth that Diana had not noticed before. As they descended the narrow path, the air grew thicker, and the smell of tobacco and wet earth filled her lungs.

They reached a kind of cave, dark but warm, where the echo of their footsteps resounded loudly. Diana felt a shiver run down her spine, not from the cold, but from the feeling that she was about to discover something that would change her life forever.

The old woman sat down on a rock at the edge of the subway stream that ran through the cave and lit another cigarette. Diana watched her in silence, waiting for the woman to speak.

-You came here because you have something inside you, something that doesn't belong to you," the old woman finally said, without looking at her.

-What am I wearing? -asked Diana, feeling that the answer would scare her.

-You carry the weight of your ancestors. Something that has been passed down from generation to generation and has haunted you to this place.

Diana swallowed saliva, feeling the pressure in her chest return.

-What should I do? -he asked, his voice trembling.

The old woman looked directly into her eyes for the first time. There was something in her gaze that made her feel naked, exposed. The woman slowly stood up and began to trace signs on the floor with something that looked like white chalk.

-You will have to face what is chasing you," the old woman replied. But you will not do it alone.

Diana watched her in silence, as the old woman continued with the ritual, her low voice echoing off the cave walls. She knew what was to come would be difficult, but she also knew it was inevitable.

The group, which had been left behind, watched Diana from a distance, perplexed by what they had just witnessed. Although they could not hear what had happened, the tension in the air was palpable. However, Diana did not stop to explain anything to them. When she returned to the group, she could barely articulate what she had felt: a mixture of terror and intrigue.

-Come on, let's go back to camp," said Alejandro, noticing the pallor on his sister's face. We'll talk about it later.

The group decided to return, in silence, as night began to fall rapidly.

Chapter 6

The Presence in the Night

The group was walking back to the camp, still in shock about what had happened. Diana walked beside Alejandro, deep in thought. She couldn't stop thinking about the old woman she had seen and what it meant. She knew that this was just the beginning of something much bigger.

Once in the camp, the tranquility they expected did not come. The night was falling quickly, enveloping them in an unsettling darkness. Alejandro lit the campfire, trying to dissipate the cold that seemed to penetrate beyond the skin.

-Are you all right, Diana? -he asked, noting her worried expression.

Diana nodded, but her mind was still caught up in the encounter. She couldn't get that experience she'd had with the old woman out of her head, that same feeling that now intensified as the shadows around the camp seemed to move with a life of their own.

Diana nodded as she settled into a folding chair near the fire. She wrapped herself in a blanket, trying to concentrate on the warmth of the fire rather than the nagging discomfort she'd been feeling since they'd been out exploring.

-Yes... just a little tired," Diana replied, but her voice betrayed the restlessness she felt. Every sound in the forest, every rustle or rustle, made her startle. She couldn't get the idea that something was watching them out of her head.

Valeria and Laura were trying to distract themselves, talking about the excursion and the photos they had taken, but even they could feel the tense atmosphere.

-Maybe we should tell a story to relax," suggested Laura, trying to lighten the mood.

Alejandro smiled, always ready to keep the group's spirits up.

-How about a horror story? We are in the perfect place for that.

Diana looked at him reproachfully but said nothing. It was not the time for jokes. However, before Alejandro could begin his story, a sudden loud sound broke the quiet of the night. It was a rustling sound as if someone or something was walking near the camp.

-Did you hear that? -asked Valeria, her voice trembling slightly.

Everyone was silent, their hearts pounding. The sound was repeated, this time closer, more definite. Diana felt the pressure in her chest intensify, her breathing became rapid and shallow.

-It must be an animal," Alejandro tried to say, although his tone did not sound very convincing.

-Yes, an animal... -Laura repeated, but no one moved. The sound had stopped, but the tension in the air was palpable. Suddenly, the campfire seemed to crackle with more intensity, casting shadows that danced strangely in the trees.

Diana could not take her eyes off the shadows. There was something about them that was not normal, something that seemed to move independently of the fire. She felt that if she blinked, she would lose sight of whatever was there, stalking them.

-We should go into the cabin," said Valeria, breaking the silence. I don't feel comfortable out here.

Alejandro nodded.

-You're right let's go inside. It's already late.

The group immediately got up, extinguishing the campfire, and gathering their things. As they made their way to the cabin, Diana couldn't help but turn her eyes one last time toward the forest. In the darkness, just at the edge where the firelight no longer reached, she swore she saw a tall, slender figure, motionless among the trees. But when she blinked, there was nothing there.

She said nothing to the others, just hurried her pace, wishing she was inside the cabin and away from the night, the shadows... and the feeling of being watched.

Once inside the cabin, the atmosphere did not improve much. Although the fire in the fireplace created a cozy warmth, the oppressive feeling in the air persisted. The windows were large, overlooking the dark forest that surrounded them, and every time someone looked out, they felt that something or someone might be watching them from the darkness.

-Why don't we watch a movie? -suggested Laura, taking out her cell phone to distract herself. That will help us relax.

Diana nodded with a forced smile, but her mind was elsewhere. Now and then, she glanced at the shadows in the corners of the cabin, waiting for something to emerge from them. Finally, the weariness of the day began to take hold of everyone, and one by one they retired to their rooms.

Diana was the last one to stay awake, staring at the flames in the fireplace that crackled hypnotically. She knew she shouldn't dwell on what had happened, but she couldn't help it. That figure in the forest, that strange presence... it all seemed more real than she was willing to admit. With a sigh, she turned off the lights in the living room and headed for her room.

The Dream Encounter

That night, Diana's dreams were dark and confused. She saw herself walking alone through the forest, listening to the whispers of the wind, but this time it wasn't just the wind. It was voices, voices that seemed to call to her from beyond the trees. She walked faster, trying to escape, but the whispers followed her. Turning a bend in the path, she saw the old woman with the tobacco again. This time, her face was clearer, and though she did not speak, her dark eyes seemed to penetrate Diana's soul.

The old woman raised her hand, pointing to something in the distance. When Diana followed the direction of her finger, she saw the cabin she was staying in, but it was no longer the same. It was old, dilapidated, and surrounded by shadows crawling across the ground, snaking toward her.

Diana awoke with a start, her heart racing. The walls of her room seemed to close in on her, and the echo of sleep still echoed in her mind. She knew she would not sleep again that night, so she got up and went to the kitchen in search of water. As she passed through the living room, she saw Alexander sitting by the fireplace, watching the embers still smoldering faintly.

-You can't sleep either? -asked Alejandro, without taking his eyes off the fire.

Diana shook her head, sitting down next to him.

-I had a strange dream... again.

Alejandro looked at her out of the corner of his eye.

-Was it about the old woman?

Diana looked at him in surprise. He hadn't told her anything about the encounter in the forest. How did he know?

-How...? -she started to ask, but Alejandro interrupted her.

-I've seen it too. I don't know what's going on, but I don't think we're alone here.

Diana felt a shiver run down her spine. She wasn't the only one who had felt something. Alexander, ever the skeptic, was beginning to believe that there was more to the place than met the eye.

-Maybe we should do more research on this mountain," Diana said quietly. I feel we are in danger, but I don't know why.

Alexander nodded slowly; his gaze lost in the embers.

-Tomorrow we will explore more. We must find out what's going on before it's too late.

Both were silent, each immersed in their thoughts. They knew the next day would bring answers, but they also feared what they might discover.

Chapter 7

The Whistle of the Mountain

The mountain was immersed in an eerie tranquility. The group, after their strange encounter with the shadows the night before, was trying to regain some semblance of normalcy. However, the atmosphere was dense and charged with a subtle tension, almost imperceptible, but palpable to those who had experienced the unknown.

Diana kept thinking about the old woman and the warnings she had felt during her dream. Although she didn't fully understand what had happened, she knew that something inside her had changed. She felt more connected to the bush, but also more vulnerable to its secrets.

-Come on, we must continue the excursion," said Alejandro, his voice firmer than usual, as if trying to convince himself that all was well.

The group nodded, but the enthusiasm of the first day was gone. The footsteps were slower and the conversations shorter. Diana remained silent; her eyes fixed on the path that led deeper into the forest. As they advanced, the sound of the wind through the leaves became deeper, like a whisper that seemed to carry words that only she could understand.

Suddenly, a high-pitched whistle echoed in the distance, cutting through the air with precision. Diana stopped dead in her tracks, her heart pounding in her chest. It wasn't just any whistle; it was something else.

-Did you hear him? -he asked in a trembling voice.

Alexander frowned, looking around. -It must be the wind," he replied, trying to sound nonchalant, but even he knew it wasn't true.

The group continued walking, but the tension increased with each step. The forest seemed thicker, darker. The shadows lengthened strangely, and the feeling of being watched grew stronger. Valeria, who was walking a few meters ahead, stopped abruptly.

-What is it? -asked Laura, coming closer.

-Over there... among the trees... -murmured Valeria, pointing with a trembling finger.

They all turned to look in the direction he pointed. At first, they saw nothing, only the darkness of the forest. But after a few seconds, something began to move in the shadows. It was a tall, slender figure, almost human, but with something strange about its silhouette. It did not walk like a person but glided smoothly through the trees as if floating.

-What... what is that? -Alejandro whispered, taking a step back.

Diana felt fear grip her body, paralyzing her. She knew they were not alone, and whatever was there was not human. The figure stopped for a moment, and although it had no face, Diana felt it was looking directly at her.

The whistling resounded again, louder this time as if coming from all directions. The wind intensified, sending leaves flying all around them. The group backed away, frightened, but something in Diana held her still. It was as if that figure was calling her as if it wanted to reveal something to her.

-Diana, let's go! -shouted Alejandro, pulling her arm.

Diana blinked, shaking off the trance she had fallen into, and followed her brother as the group ran back to camp. But even as they tried to escape, the whistling sound followed them, echoing in their ears like a distant but constant echo.

When they finally reached the cabin, they slammed the door shut, trying to catch their breath. Alejandro lit the fireplace, his hands shaking.

-What the hell was that? -asked Valeria, her voice broken with fear.

No one answered. Silence fell again, interrupted only by the crackling of the fire. Diana sat in one of the chairs, staring at the ground. She knew the bush was warning them of something, but she didn't know what.

That night, while everyone was trying to sleep, Diana heard the whistling again, soft, but unmistakable. This time, she didn't try to ignore it. She knew it wouldn't end until she discovered what the bush wanted to show her.

Chapter 8

The old lady

The restlessness she had felt since the beginning of the trip had not disappeared but had transformed into an uncontrollable need. Despite what had happened in the forest, Diana knew she had to return. Something was calling her back, something she had not yet fully discovered.

-You can't be serious, Diana," said Alejandro, when she mentioned the idea of going back to the bush.

-I must. I don't know how to explain it, but... I feel that if I don't go back, something bad is going to happen," she answered firmly, her voice more confident than she felt.

Alexander frowned, looking at his sister. He knew Diana didn't take these things lightly, but he also knew that what they were facing was more than either of them could comprehend.

Despite Alejandro's warnings, Diana decided to go. Dusk was already upon them when she entered the forest, following the same path that had led her to the strange experience on the mountain the first time. The sunlight was gradually disappearing, enveloping the forest in a twilight that seemed to distort reality.

She climbed the mountain with determined steps, the twilight enveloping the landscape in a dim light. The clarity of the stream soon appeared in front of her, and as before, the elders were already there, dressed in white, as if they had been waiting for her. The man, with his lighted tobacco, cast an approving glance, while the old woman drew symbols on the ground with white chalk.

One of the elders extended his hand, signaling Diana to kneel. She obeyed without question, knowing that this moment was crucial.

-You are ready to free yourself completely from what binds you," said the old man, his voice firm but calm.

The man blew the tobacco smoke around Diana, while the old woman poured brandy on the floor and made symbols with something that looked like white chalk. The scent of candle and brandy was strong, and enveloping, and although Diana had felt fear before, this time she experienced only a deep calm.

-What you carry inside you is not yours alone," the old woman continued. You have taken the weight of your ancestors, their mistakes, and their suffering. Today, we free you.

The elders' chants rose, their voices soft but powerful, as the symbols on the ground seemed to glow in the moonlight. Diana closed her eyes, letting a sense of relief and release wash over her. The shadows that had once tormented her seemed to disappear, and the pain she had felt since they arrived on the mountain dissipated.

When the chanting stopped, Diana slowly opened her eyes. The elders were watching her with a quiet smile.

-You have broken the cycle, the evil of your ancestors," said the old woman. The shadows of your dead relatives will no longer follow you. You are free.

Diana felt an indescribable peace. She knew she had faced something greater than she could comprehend, but she also knew she had made it through. She stood up, grateful, and looked at the elders one last time before their figures began to fade into the darkness.

She returned to the cabin, where her friends and brother were waiting for her. When she entered, Alejandro quickly got up and approached her with a mixture of concern and relief.

-Where have you been? -he asked, though his eyes seemed to understand more than his words suggested.

Diana tried to explain to him what she had experienced, but words did not seem enough. Alexander, however, nodded silently, as if he knew that what his sister had experienced was beyond what any logical explanation could encompass.

That night, while the others slept, Alejandro sat down next to Diana and, in a low tone, confessed to her something he had been holding back.

-I've heard stories of this place... of people who have disappeared and come back, but they are never the same. I think what happened to you is beyond what we understand.

Diana felt a chill as she listened to her brother's words. She knew they could not stay any longer on Mount Prisank, but she also understood that what she had experienced would not stay there. The shadows she had faced, the rituals she had witnessed, it was all part of something much bigger, something she was just beginning to understand.

Chapter 9

Revelation in the Clear

Diana returned to the cabin, more serene after the ritual with the elders. The weight she felt in her soul had disappeared, and although she could not fully explain it, she knew that something profound had changed. Alexander noticed something different about her; her eyes looked clear, but her mind was still distant as if part of her remained connected to Mount Prisank.

The next morning came with a strange calm. However, there was a tension in the air that no one could ignore. Despite the tranquility Diana felt after the ritual, the atmosphere felt charged, as if something invisible was watching them.

Alejandro, concerned about his sister's reserved behavior, decided to talk to her. They sat in silence by the cabin while the rest of the group continued their day as if nothing had happened.

-Diana, what happened last night? -asked Alejandro, his tone full of concern. What we are experiencing is not normal.

Diana looked out into the forest, pensive, as if trying to process what she had experienced.

-It's not easy to explain," he finally replied. The elders freed me from something... something I didn't even know was there. But I don't think this is over. There's something else we need to find out.

Alejandro felt a shiver. Diana's words unsettled him more than he wanted to admit. As they spoke, a strange sound interrupted their conversation: distant, childish laughter, like that of a child playing in the forest. It was a sound that did not belong to that place or that moment.

-Did you hear that? -asked Alejandro, standing up immediately.

Diana nodded silently, but she didn't look surprised. There was something in her face that indicated she was already expecting it. Without a second thought, they started walking towards the sound, not knowing what they would find. The forest seemed thicker, the shadows lengthened strangely, and the air grew colder as they advanced.

The laughter was repeated, this time closer. Alexander looked around nervously, but Diana remained calm as if she knew where the laughter was leading them. Finally, they reached the clearing where, the night before, Diana had found the elders. The place was deserted, but the laughter persisted, bouncing through the trees.

-We are not alone, Alejandro," Diana said, her voice steady. There is something here, something that does not belong to this world.

Alexander swallowed hard. The clearing seemed to be shrouded in a fog that had not been there before, and although they could see no one, they could both sense the presence of something watching them.

-What do we do now? -asked Alejandro, his voice trembling.

-I don't know, but I think we have no choice but to face whatever is following us," Diana replied, with a determination that frightened her brother.

Suddenly, a gust of wind shook the tree branches and with it, the laughter vanished into thin air. Instead, a deafening silence enveloped them. Diana took a deep breath, closing her eyes for a moment, seeking clarity amidst the chaos she felt.

The wind brought with it a distant murmur, but this time, it wasn't laughter. Alexander looked at his sister, waiting for her to take the initiative. Before she could react, they both saw something in the trees: a small, dark figure moving slowly toward them.

Alejandro felt his legs weaken. Diana, on the other hand, did not take her eyes off the figure, as if something inside her was telling her that she should not move.

-He's coming towards us," whispered Alejandro, unable to hide the fear in his voice.

Diana said nothing. The figure stopped a few meters away from them, but the fog enveloped her so much that they could not clearly distinguish her features. They only knew that she was not alone. Behind her, the shadows began to move eerily, as if they were alive, watching her every move.

-Diana, let's get out of here. This... this is not right," Alejandro insisted, gently pulling his sister's hand.

But Diana did not move. She kept her gaze fixed on the figure, waiting for something as if she knew that this moment was crucial.

-I can't leave," he finally said. This is part of what we must face.

Alexander felt a shiver run down his spine. He did not understand what Diana was saying, but he knew they were in danger. However, something in his sister prevented him from moving, as if she was somehow connected to what was happening.

Suddenly, the dark figure took a step toward them, and in that instant, Alexander knew they could not stay any longer. He grabbed Diana by the arm and forced her back, slowly moving away from the clearing.

As they moved away, the figure faded into the fog, but the shadows continued to move around them. Alexander's breath hitched, feeling the terror grow with each step they took toward the safety of the cabin.

Finally reaching the cabin, they closed the door behind them, trying to catch their breath. Diana remained silent, looking out the window at the forest.

-This is not over," he said quietly. Whatever is on Mount Prisank won't let us go so easily.

Alejandro did not answer. He knew Diana was right, but the fear of the unknown was all over him. He knew the worst was yet to come.

Chapter 10

The Secret Revealed

The icy wind that enveloped the mountain seemed to intensify as Diana and Alejandro advanced. The children's distant laughter continued to echo, softer and softer, like a fading echo through the trees. But there was something in that laughter that they could not ignore, an oppressive sensation that made them feel that they were being watched from every angle. Alexander shuddered as he remembered the faint figure, they had spotted moments before, the small shadow that seemed to move through the trees and disappear before they could make it out clearly.

-Are you sure we should go ahead? -Alexander asked, his voice barely a whisper as he cautiously scanned the surroundings.

-We have no choice," Diana replied, her tone calm but determined. Something inside her was pushing her forward as if she knew she had to face whatever awaited them on that mountain.

The trees stood tall and dark around them, like silent guardians of a secret that had remained hidden for generations. The path, which once seemed clear, now became more winding and closed, as if the mountain itself was trying to confuse them. Despite the growing darkness, Diana walked steadily, guided by a force that even she did not fully understand.

The silence that surrounded them was disturbing. They could no longer hear the wind or the rustle of the trees, as if the forest had decided to hold its breath in their presence. Alejandro tried to distract himself by looking at the leaves beneath his feet, but his mind kept returning to the image of the boy they had briefly seen small, dark, dressed in red and black. Although they had barely been able to make out his features, the feeling that he was more than just a child was undeniable.

-Did you see the boy well? -asked Alejandro, his voice sounding tense. Diana nodded silently but did not comment. The child was not what worried her most. Her intuition told her that there was something much deeper and more dangerous lurking in that mountain, something that went beyond the laughter of a lost spirit.

Suddenly, something in the air changed. The atmosphere became heavier, as if an invisible presence was hovering over them. Diana stopped dead in her tracks, her eyes focused on something Alexander could not see. Ahead of them, the path opened into a clearing. On the ground, among the dry leaves and dirt, were symbols painted in what appeared to be white chalk. They were strange, and tangled, as if representing distorted human figures or endless spirals. The air around these symbols felt charged as if the unseen observers Alexander so feared had decided to show their presence more tangibly.

-What is this? -Alejandro muttered, bending down to take a closer look at the symbols.

-Don't touch it," Diana warned, her voice cutting. She felt that those symbols were not there by chance. There was something ritualistic about them as if they had been left there to keep forces, she couldn't even understand at bay.

Alejandro stood up slowly, his face pale. Although he didn't believe in the supernatural in the same way his sister did, he knew they shouldn't keep playing with something they didn't understand. A whisper, like a light breeze, drifted across the clearing, carrying with it an incomprehensible murmur that seemed to come from the trees themselves.

-You heard that, didn't you? -asked Alejandro, his anxious gaze searching for Diana's approval.

She nodded again but didn't move. She knew they were about to discover something that would change everything. But what she didn't know was whether they were ready to face it. Suddenly, a sound of footsteps crunched behind them. They both turned in unison but saw no one. However, the feeling of being watched increased, as if something or someone was silently surrounding them, waiting for the right moment to show itself.

Without a word, they both started walking again, their bodies tense, their hearts pounding. The path led them deeper into the forest, until, in the distance, they saw the entrance to a cave. Daylight barely filtered through the clouds, and the cave seemed dark and silent, like an open mouth waiting to devour them.

-Diana... we shouldn't go in there," said Alejandro, his voice trembling.

-We have no choice," Diana replied, her gaze fixed on the darkness that beckoned them from inside the cave.

They both knew that this cave was no ordinary place. The cave had an aura of mystery as if the walls held ancient secrets that should not be discovered. As they went deeper, the air changed again, becoming thicker, and colder. But what disturbed them most was the absolute silence. Not even the echo of their footsteps echoed off the stone walls.

As they advanced in the gloom, they saw a dim light in the background. Once they reached the end of the cave, the light came from candles placed around a small altar. And there stood the elders, the same ones they had seen before, chanting in deep, dark whispers. Their movements were rapid, their hands gestured as if they were invoking something, something that seemed to float between reality and dream.

Alexander felt a shiver run down his spine as one of the elders looked directly at him. It was as if he could see right through him as if he knew his deepest fears and secrets.

-The price will be paid..." the elders muttered in unison, without stopping moving. Diana felt her blood run cold at those words. She knew the price they spoke of was not something they could avoid.

-What are you talking about? -asked Alejandro, with a mixture of desperation and confusion.

The elders did not respond, they only continued with their chanting. But Diana understood, at that very moment, that the price they were talking about was not for them. Something or someone had to be sacrificed so that they could return safely from that cursed place.

Without a word, Diana took Alexander's hand, and they began to back away slowly, their hearts beating wildly. The elders did not attempt to stop them, but the whisper of their words continued to fill the cave: **"The price will be paid.... the price will be paid..."**

Finally, they reached the exit of the cave, the cold air outside hitting their faces like a slap of reality. They both knew that the forest was no longer the same for them. The shadows lengthened strangely, the sounds of the wind seemed to form words they could not understand, and that oppressive feeling of being watched intensified with every step they took.

The trip back to the cabin was silent. Neither dared speak of what had happened, but both knew that something dark and ancient had been unleashed. What they didn't know was whether it was too late to stop it.

Chapter 11

The Final Decision

Night covered the forest with a palpable darkness. Diana and Alejandro, after leaving the cave, felt a strange weight on them as they made their way back to the cabin. Although they were closer to civilization, the sense of danger was still present. The words of the elders echoed in their minds: "The price will be paid."

Alejandro, still shaken by what he had experienced, tried to remain calm. The images of the boy dressed in red and black, small, and blurry, were still in his head. He knew there was something darker behind that figure, something they still did not understand.

-Diana, what do you think they meant by the price? -asked Alejandro, trying to understand what was in store for them.

Diana took a deep breath before responding as if searching for a way to verbalize what she was feeling.

-I don't know, but I think we'll find out soon. This is not over," he replied, with an eerie calm.

Alexander shuddered, sensing that something greater was at stake. As they advanced, the air seemed to grow thicker, as if the mountain itself was watching them. The moon, barely visible, cast elongated, misshapen shadows around them, fueling the growing sense of danger.

When they finally arrived at the cabin, Valeria and Laura were outside, visibly worried.

-Where the hell were you? -shouted Valeria, running towards them, "We've been worried for hours!

Alexander tried to calm her with a strained smile, but before he could explain himself, a loud metallic noise echoed through the forest, freezing them in place.

-What was that? -asked Laura, trembling.

Diana looked out into the forest; her eyes narrowed as if waiting for something to emerge from the shadows.

-We are not alone," he said, his voice low but firm.

The four looked at each other in silence, sensing something lurking in the darkness. They quickly entered the cabin, closing the door behind them. Despite being safely inside, the tension did not disappear.

Alejandro broke the silence.

-We should get out of here... right now," he said with an urgent tone.

-We can't," Diana replied, her gaze fixed on the window. Not until we find out what's going on.

-To discover what? This doesn't make sense! -We are being stalked by something we can't even see!

-This goes beyond us," Diana replied, not looking away from the darkness. It's not just about what's going on here... there's something deeper.

Suddenly, a sharp knock sounded at the door, freezing everyone's blood. Valeria and Laura looked at each other in terror. The knock was repeated this time with more force.

-Don't open," whispered Valeria, clinging to Laura.

-I'm not going to do it," Alejandro answered, his voice trembling.

The knock echoed once more, and suddenly the air in the hut changed. A chill invaded the space, and a barely perceptible whisper began to fill everything. It was as if the walls themselves were speaking in an ancient and forgotten language.

Diana cautiously approached the window and saw him: the dark-haired boy in red and black, motionless, just outside the cabin, watching them from a distance.

-It's him... -Diana murmured.

-Who? -asked Laura, frightened.

-The boy we saw in the forest. He's here... just outside.

The silence became thick, almost unbearable. None of them could move. Alejandro, not knowing what else to do, approached the door and, very carefully, slowly opened it. But there was no one outside. Only the blackness of the forest and the wind whispering through the trees.

-There is no one... -said Alejandro, visibly disconcerted.

Diana, however, knew that this was not over.

-He's playing with us.... -he muttered; his eyes fixed on the dark horizon.

The night was endless. None of them could sleep, every creak, and every sound of the wind made them jump. Fear had them trapped. They knew something darker was stalking them, something that would not stop until it got what it wanted.

When dawn finally began to light up the sky, Diana and Alejandro felt a little safer, but the relief was momentary. They decided to venture back into the forest, searching for answers. They walked in silence until they came to a clearing.

There, their mother was waiting for them, but something in her face was distorted as if she didn't quite belong in this world.

-Mom..." Diana whispered, her voice trembling.

Diana's mother approached slowly, but in her eyes, there was a deep sadness. At that moment, Diana understood that the price the elders mentioned was not abstract. Something or someone had to pay for it.

-She... She's not here," said Alejandro, stepping back. She's not our mother. This is an illusion.

Before they could process it, everything changed. The sound of sirens filled the air. Diana opened her eyes and saw the clear sky above her. She was alive. Alejandro, next to her, was being attended to by paramedics.

-Diana! -cried her mother, running to her, "We thought we'd lost you!

Diana, hugging her mother, felt a deep emptiness. Looking around, she saw her friends crying, some in shock. But something else had happened.

-Mom..." she whispered, trying to hold back her tears. You don't know what we've been through.

One of their friends lay lifeless on a stretcher. Someone else had paid the price so that they could return.

Chapter 12

Incomplete Cycles

Months later, back in the city, Diana and Alejandro's life had been completely transformed. Although physically present, they felt that part of them had remained in the mountain. The smell of tobacco followed them, like a persistent reminder that something was not over. The death of their friend weighed on them, a guilt Diana could not ignore. The scent, unmistakable, appeared in unexpected places: her apartment, the street, and even at work. Every day she felt more and more trapped in a kind of emotional limbo, where reality and the mountain experience began to blend.

Alejandro, for his part, was trying to get back to normal, but his attempts to talk about what happened only led to isolation. No one understood, no one could grasp the truth of what had happened. In everyone's eyes, they had found them just in time. But Alejandro knew, as did Diana, that they had died, and that someone else had paid the price for their return.

The tobacco, the sound of the wind, the shadows in the window reflections. Everything seemed to indicate that the mountain was following them, that they had not completely escaped. Diana remembered her dead friend with a mixture of sadness and resignation, wondering if that price should have been paid for her. Guilt was becoming her constant companion; one she could not leave behind.

One afternoon, as they were walking through the city, Diana stopped abruptly in front of a store. In the reflection of the glass, she saw him. One of the elders was standing, watching her, with the same calm and enigmatic expression he had had in the cave. She turned immediately, but no one was there. Alejandro, noticing her reaction, looked at his sister.

-Did you see it? -asked Diana, her heart racing.

Alejandro nodded slowly. It was not a hallucination; they both knew that. Even though they were trying to leave Mount Prisank behind, their connection to the elders was still present. The cycle had never closed.

The weeks continued, but the discomfort only grew. Diana began to have more recurring dreams of the elderly, in which they spoke to her in a language she did not understand. Every time she woke up, the smell of tobacco was there, lingering, as if something was trying to lure her back.

One day, to deal with her grief, Diana decided to visit the cemetery where her friend was buried. The flowers she brought seemed to wilt as soon as she placed them on the grave. She knelt in silence, tears streaming down her face. Alejandro, always nearby, watched her from a few steps behind, without saying a word.

-I can't go on like this," Diana finally said, between sobs. She died for us. I feel I don't deserve to be here.

Alexander crouched down next to her, gently touching her shoulder.

-It wasn't your fault. None of us understood what was going on," he replied, his voice cracking with emotion.

As they got up to leave, Diana noticed something strange. On her friend's grave, there was a small tobacco cigarette, barely lit. There was no one around, but the smell was unmistakable. Alejandro also saw it and instinctively stepped back.

-This is not over," said Alejandro, in a barely audible whisper. The price is still pending.

The following weeks became a constant struggle to maintain their sanity. Both were trying to resume their routines, but they knew that something unseen was haunting them. The cycle they were part of was still incomplete as if the world they had touched on the mountain was pulling at them again.

One night, while Diana was alone in her apartment, she heard a whisper in the air. She looked around but saw no one. She closed her eyes, breathing deeply, when the smell of tobacco became unbearably strong. He opened his eyes quickly and there, across the room, he saw the figure of the boy, just as he had seen him on the mountain, dressed in red and black. He had no fear, only immense sadness.

-Why are you following me? -he asked, almost in despair.

The boy did not answer, just watched her with his calm expression, as if he expected something from her. Diana, finally, understood. It was not the end, the cycle had to continue, and if they were alive, that connection with Mount Prisank would still be present, dragging them always into the shadows.

Life went on for both, but always with the latent presence of that other world. The price for returning had never quite been completed, and although the elders and the child did not haunt them in a threatening way, their constant presence was a reminder that, at some point, the cycle had to close.

Alexander and Diana accepted that reality. They knew they were not alone, that what they had experienced on Mount Prisank would stay with them forever. Sometimes, amidst the bustle of the city, Diana could smell the tobacco, and see the shadows move around her, and in those moments, she felt that everything was closer than it seemed. But what she didn't know was when, or how, the cycle would finally end.

-The cycle never closes completely," Alejandro would murmur from time to time as if that phrase had become his mantra.

And with that uncertainty, they lived from day to day, knowing that the mountain, the elders, the child, and the shadows would always be there, waiting.

61

Chapter 13

The Mystery of the Unknown Language

It was a quiet night when everything changed for Diana. Alejandro, her mother, and she were at the table, enjoying a home-cooked dinner. The conversation was flowing casually, but suddenly, the atmosphere became strange. Diana, who was eating quietly, dropped her fork and froze.

-Diana, are you all, right? -asked Alejandro, noticing the change in his sister's face.

Before he could respond, he began to tremble. He closed his eyes and words began to come out of his mouth that they did not understand. It sounded like an ancient language, something none of them had ever heard before. His mother got up from her chair in fright.

-Diana! -he shouted, as he ran to her to hold her.

But Diana kept talking, her voice sounding louder, as if she were repeating a message coming from somewhere else. Fear gripped the room. Alejandro tried to calm her down, but the more he did so, the more intense the trembling became.

Finally, not knowing what else to do, her mother decided to take her to the hospital. Alejandro helped her into the car while she continued to mumble incomprehensible words. During the drive, the atmosphere was charged with tension, and they both wondered what was going on with Diana.

At the hospital, the doctors examined her immediately. They ran tests, looking for some logical explanation for what had happened. But the results were surprising.

-She is completely healthy," said one of the doctors, unable to find anything unusual. There is no physical reason for what they describe.

Alejandro and his mother looked at each other in confusion. How could he be okay if they had just witnessed something so strange?

Hours later, when Diana woke up in the clinic, she was already calm. Alejandro and her mother looked at her with relief, but also with many questions.

-What happened? -asked Alejandro, sitting down next to her.

Diana looked at them, clearly confused.

-I don't know," he said quietly. I was eating, and suddenly I felt a shiver all over my body as if something was running through me from head to toe. Then a choking in the pit of my stomach... and from there I don't remember anything until now.

None of them knew what to say. Something had happened something beyond their comprehension, but they did not know how to deal with it. Uncertainty accompanied them back home, where silence settled in every corner.

Chapter 14

The Store

A few weeks later, things seemed to have returned to normal. Diana tried not to think too much about the episode in the hospital, although from time to time, she felt that same strange sensation in her body. However, everything changed again one day when they went shopping.

They were in a local store, looking for some clothes, when an older lady, who worked there, approached them unexpectedly. She was wearing a simple dress, but her eyes seemed to see beyond what was in front of her.

-They must finish what they started," he said, staring at them.

Alejandro froze. What was he talking about? Neither he nor Diana had said anything to anyone about what had happened, much less to a stranger.

-Excuse me, what do you mean? -asked Alejandro, trying to sound calm, although the uneasiness in his voice was evident.

The lady did not answer directly. She just handed them a small piece of paper with a written address and, before walking away, she said:

-Do not be afraid. Go and you will understand.

Diana and Alejandro stood there, staring at the address, both feeling a mixture of curiosity and fear. They both felt a mixture of curiosity and fear. What did it all mean? Why was a stranger giving them such a disturbing address and message?

-What do we do? -asked Diana, holding the paper in her hand.

-I don't know if we should go," said Alejandro, clearly nervous. I don't have a good feeling about this.

But curiosity soon overcame fear. Alejandro knew that if they didn't investigate, they would never get answers about what had happened to his sister. With some trepidation, they decided to follow the address.

When they arrived, they found a small, modest house with a humble facade. But as soon as they entered the house, the atmosphere changed. The interior of the house was surprisingly bright and welcoming, with a peace that contrasted with the plain exterior. They were greeted by a modest-looking family but with an almost spiritual tranquility in their mannerisms.

-Hello, welcome," said one of them, inviting them to sit down.

The family did not ask them direct questions but seemed to know what had brought them there. During a long talk, they spoke of energies, of how people can get caught between invisible forces. They did not mention religions but spoke of a "path" Diana and Alejandro were to follow, a higher step in their spiritual journey.

-They need not fear," said the older woman in the family. But they must be ready for what is coming.

You have been called to something greater, something you may not yet fully understand. But if you wish to understand, you must stay here with us for three days.

Alejandro exchanged a glance with Diana, clearly uneasy.

-Stay? -asked Alejandro, trying to remain calm. What does that mean?

The older woman did not look away from them. Her expression was calm, but her words were filled with a certainty that made it impossible to ignore.

-It will be three days," he continued. During that time, you may not leave this house or have contact with the outside world. You must not tell anyone what you will do here, or what you will learn. This is a process of transformation, and it requires your total dedication.

Diana felt a knot in her stomach. Something about this proposal seemed to defy logic, but at the same time, the idea of finding out what was going on in her life was too strong to refuse.

-What should we bring? -she asked, surprised that her own words had come out so quickly.

The woman smiled softly as if she was already expecting that answer.

-Nothing but yourselves," he replied. What you need you will find here. But you must be sure of your decision. Once you cross this threshold to begin, there will be no turning back until the three days are over.

Alexander looked at his sister, doubt written on his face.

-Diana, I don't know if we should do this. -he murmured to make her reconsider.

But Diana had already made up her mind. What had happened to her, the episode at the hospital, and the strange feeling of being connected to something else, all pushed her forward. She needed answers.

-Let's do it," he finally said, with a conviction that surprised his brother.

The family rose slowly as if Diana's decision had sealed a silent pact.

-All right," said the oldest man in the family. We'll start tomorrow at dawn. You must not tell anyone about what will happen here. This is a journey between you, and us and what lies beyond. Do not fear, but do not underestimate what is to come.

With those words, the meeting ended. Diana and Alejandro left the house with the feeling that they had just taken the first step towards something much deeper. They knew that when they returned the next morning, nothing would ever be the same again.

The darkness of the night enveloped the way back, and although the streets were silent, the echo of the family's words echoed in both of their minds. Diana, though frightened, felt closer to understanding what was happening in her life. Alejandro, though doubtful, knew they could no longer back out.

The three days ahead would be a challenge, but also an opportunity to understand that invisible legacy that followed them. And though they didn't know what to expect, they knew they were prepared to face it, together.

Chapter 15

The Three Days

Day 1: The Language of the Soul

The first day began with an eerie calm. Diana and Alejandro, after accepting the family's invitation, found themselves in a simple room, but imbued with an energy that neither could describe. The family wasted no time, and, after a light meal, they were ushered into a small room filled with candles and earthenware bowls emanating an incense aroma.

-Today we will begin to teach you the language of the soul," said the older woman, who seemed to be leading the group. It is not a language you can learn with words. It is deeper, beyond what you can understand with your mind. It is a language you must feel with your heart.

Diana and Alejandro sat across from the old woman. Around them, the walls seemed to vibrate softly, as if the air was alive. The woman began to recite words in a strange language, something neither Diana nor Alejandro had ever heard before. They were soft sounds, almost sung, but at the same time full of an indescribable strength.

-Repeat after me," the woman told them.

Diana and Alejandro, hesitant at first, began to imitate the sounds. At first, they found it difficult to follow the rhythm and cadence of the language, but little by little something inside them began to connect. It was as if those ancient words touched a deep part of their souls, a part that had been dormant for years.

-This language is the bridge between the visible and the invisible," the woman explained, her voice calm but firm. Speak it not with your mind, but with your spirit. It will help you communicate and direct the energies you will encounter on your path.

For the rest of the day, they practiced that language. As the day progressed, Diana noticed that the words flowed more naturally, as if they had always been inside her. Alejandro, though still skeptical, also felt something change inside him. It was not just the learning of strange sounds, it was the opening to something much deeper, something they could not explain.

When night fell, they retired to sleep, with the feeling that the next day would bring more answers.

Day 2: Cleaning and Protection

The second day began early, with the sound of birds singing outside the house. The family woke them up at dawn and, after a light breakfast, they took them to the backyard, a place surrounded by plants and flowers that seemed to vibrate with energy.

-Today you will learn to clean and protect yourselves," said the older man, who had spoken little up to that point. Not everything you feel is in your favor. Some energies are unwelcome, and you must learn to manage them.

They were handed small bundles of dried herbs, which they were to burn slowly as they walked around the courtyard. With each step, smoke filled the air, and with it, the older man recited phrases in the same language they had learned the day before. These phrases were like a prayer, but not a religious one. It was more like an invocation, a call to cleanse what should not remain.

-Every place has energies; some are ancient, and some are more recent. But when you feel something is wrong, when the shadows seem too long, that's when you should use this," he said, handing them a bowl full of salt and a small jar of oil. These are symbols of purity. Use them to mark boundaries and to protect yourselves from what you cannot see.

Diana followed each step precisely. She remembered the strange episode at the hospital, and somehow knew that what they were learning now would have helped her then. The act of cleansing, not only physically, but spiritually, had immense power she had never considered before.

During the afternoon, they were taught how to recognize negative energies. The family explained that not everything that cannot be seen is bad, but some unwanted presences manifest themselves in the form of dense air, an unexplained feeling of cold or, in some cases, as shadows in the corners of rooms.

-When you feel something is not right," the older woman explained, "use what you have learned. But remember, don't do it in fear. If you face the dark with fear, you will only feed it.

That night, after the cleansings and protections, Diana felt a peace she had not felt in a long time. It seemed as if, for the first time, she could control her surroundings. Alexander, though still somewhat skeptical, also began to understand that there was more to this world than he had once believed.

Day 3: The Celebration of Change

The third day was different. It did not begin with exercises or prayers. When they woke up, the family led them to the courtyard where they had worked the day before, but this time, it was decorated with candles, flowers and small colorful ribbons hanging from the trees.

-Today we celebrate what you have become," said the older woman, smiling for the first time with a warmth that filled the air. You have stepped into something few understand, and now you are part of something bigger.

The family received them in what appeared to be a small ceremony. There were no long speeches or detailed explanations.

It was simply an acknowledgement of what Diana and Alejandro had learned in those days. It was not something visible, but the internal changes they had experienced were profound.

-You have learned to control energies, to speak to the soul, and to protect yourselves and others," said the older man. It is not a gift to be taken lightly. What you have learned can help others, but it also carries a responsibility.

The afternoon was quiet, almost as if the celebration was more internal than external. As the day progressed, Diana and Alejandro reflected on all that they had experienced. They knew they would not be the same when they left that house, and that gave them a mixture of tranquility and respect.

Before leaving, the older woman gave them each a small candle and a bottle of oil.

-Don't forget what you learned here," he told them. If you ever feel you need to come back, this place will always be open to you.

Diana and Alejandro left at sunset, with a sense of peace and change. They knew that what had begun in that house was not the end, but only the beginning of a deeper journey.

Chapter 16

The Complete Cycle

Decades later, Diana was already an old woman. Her life had changed enormously since that experience with Alexander. Her children were grown, and her mother, who had once accompanied her on that spiritual journey, had passed away. Time had passed, but not without leaving a deep mark on Diana.

She lived in a small house, surrounded by her memories and her children who now cared for her. Her hair was gray, and her hands were wrinkled, but her eyes still shone with the same light of wisdom she had begun to develop all those years ago. Sometimes, when she looked in the mirror, she remembered the old woman she had seen on the mountain, and suddenly it all made sense.

-It's me," she whispered to herself. It was always me.

She had understood that the old woman who spoke to her and taught her about energies, who guided her on her spiritual journey, was not a mere stranger. She was a projection of what she herself would become. It was her future, her destiny. The cycle of wisdom, of connection with the unseen, had passed from generation to generation, and now she was the one who carried it.

Diana had never spoken openly with her children about what she had learned, but they knew their mother had something special. There was a peace in her presence, a calm that seemed to radiate from within her.

-Mom always knows when something isn't right," her children said, half-jokingly, half seriously.

Over time, Diana began to prepare her children, albeit subtly. She did not put them through the same rigorous training she had experienced, but she taught them to listen to their intuition, to trust the signs of the unseen world and not to fear what they could not see.

One afternoon, as the sun was setting behind the mountains, one of his sons approached him.

-Mom, sometimes I feel things... things I don't understand. Do you think that's normal? -she asked with a mixture of doubt and curiosity.

Diana smiled, recognizing the same feeling she had had so many years before.

-Yes, it's normal. What you feel is part of something bigger. One day you'll understand better," he replied calmly.

She had come to accept her role as the bearer of an ancient legacy, and while she knew that not all of her children would follow that path, one of them would. The cycle would continue.

That night, before going to bed, Diana looked in the mirror one more time. This time she saw not just an old woman, but the figure she had seen on the mountain. The woman she knew, from the beginning, she had always been meant to be. The cycle had closed, and she had fulfilled her purpose.

And as the shadows of night lengthened outside her window, Diana felt a deep peace. She had guided her family and now, finally, she could rest.

Epilogue

The Shadow of Oblivion

Years have passed since Diana and Alejandro left behind that house and the teachings, they received during those three days. However, the echo of what they learned continues to resonate in their lives. Although daily life has taken its course, the spiritual and the invisible remain a constant part of their existence.

Diana, now an old woman, has lived with the certainty that everything that happened in those days completely transformed her. Over time, she has come to understand that the knowledge that was passed on to her was not just for her, but to be passed on to the next generation, just as the family that took them in had done before. That legacy was to continue, albeit silently, unseen and misunderstood by all.

Diana often sits in the garden of her home, watching the sky and the mountains in the distance. Her children surround her, but despite the family bustle, her mind sometimes travels back to those moments on the mountain and in the family home. She knows she has become the figure she once saw, the old woman who guided her younger self. She understood that the cycle, which seemed to have begun long before she was aware of it, had transformed her, and now it was her turn to guide and protect her own.

Alejandro, for his part, has found peace in everyday life, but at times he also feels that the shadows of what they lived through still follow him. Although he no longer fears the unknown, he knows that what they learned was only a doorway to something bigger. He doesn't talk much about those days, but there are moments when he exchanges a glance with his sister and they both know that the link to the unseen is still present.

One afternoon, while walking together through the city, Diana and Alejandro stopped in front of a dark alley. In the shadows, they saw a familiar figure. It was one of the elders who had guided them so many years before, smiling silently from a distance. There was no longer fear, only a sense of calm as if the cycle had been fulfilled.

Diana, now with a wisdom she had taken a lifetime to understand, smiled to herself. She knew that the road they had traveled had not been easy, but that everything that happened had a greater purpose. The elders had always been there, not to haunt them, but to remind them that the doors to the unseen are never completely closed.

"Maybe some cycles are not broken," she thought, as the figure faded into the mist. The wind blew gently as if caressing her memories, and with a sigh, she knew that, though some doors remained ajar, she was now the guardian of that threshold.

With that certainty, Diana and Alejandro continued their way, knowing that the cycle had been fulfilled, but also with the understanding that what they learned would live on in the generations to come. The invisible energies would still be there, waiting to be discovered, guided, and understood by those who, like them, would one day be called to see beyond what the eyes can perceive.

www.ingramcontent.com/pod-product-compliance
Lightning Source LLC
Chambersburg PA
CBHW060218170726
48004CB00014B/605